JJ   Rockwell, Anne

    The Emergency Room

THE EMERGENCY ROOM

Anne & Harlow Rockwell

MACMILLAN PUBLISHING COMPANY · NEW YORK

COLLIER MACMILLAN PUBLISHERS · LONDON

Macmillan Publishing Company
866 Third Avenue, New York, N.Y. 10022
Collier Macmillan Canada, Inc.
Printed in the United States of America
10   9   8   7   6   5   4   3   2
Library of Congress Cataloging in Publication Data
Rockwell, Anne F.
The emergency room.
Summary: Explores the equipment and procedures of a
hospital emergency room by describing what one patient
sees while being treated for a sprained ankle.
1. Hospitals—Emergency service—Juvenile literature.
2. Emergency medical services—Juvenile literature.
[1. Hospitals—Emergency service.   2. Emergency medical
services]   I. Rockwell, Harlow.   II. Title.
RA975.E5R63 1985   362.1'8   84-20161
ISBN 0- 02-777300-0

The emergency room is at the hospital.
People go there when they are hurt or very sick.

Sometimes
ambulances bring them.
Doctors and nurses work
at the emergency room
day and night.

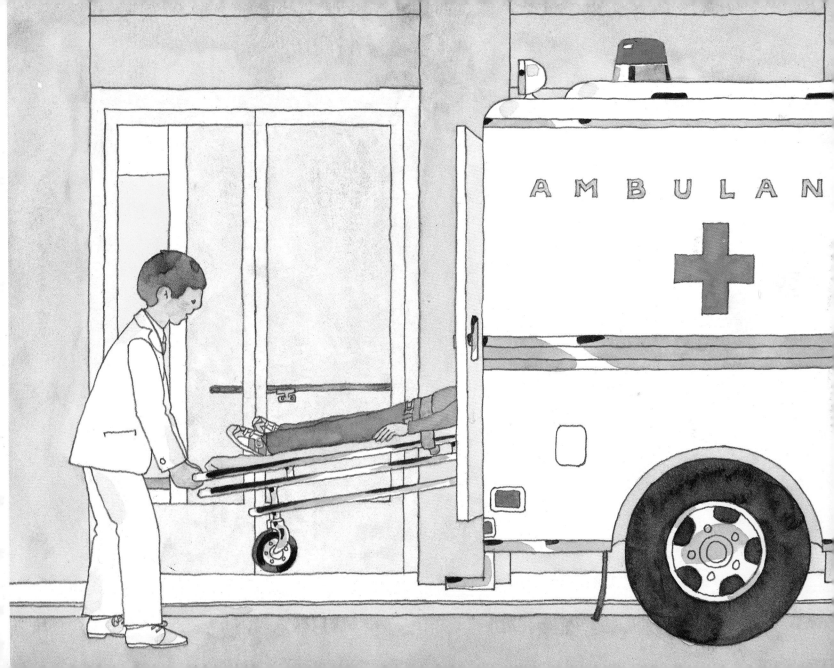

There are wheelchairs

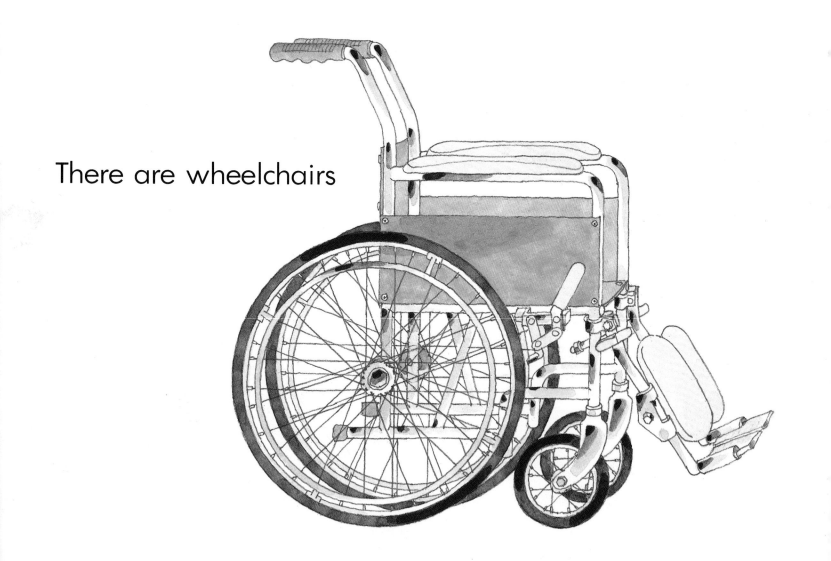

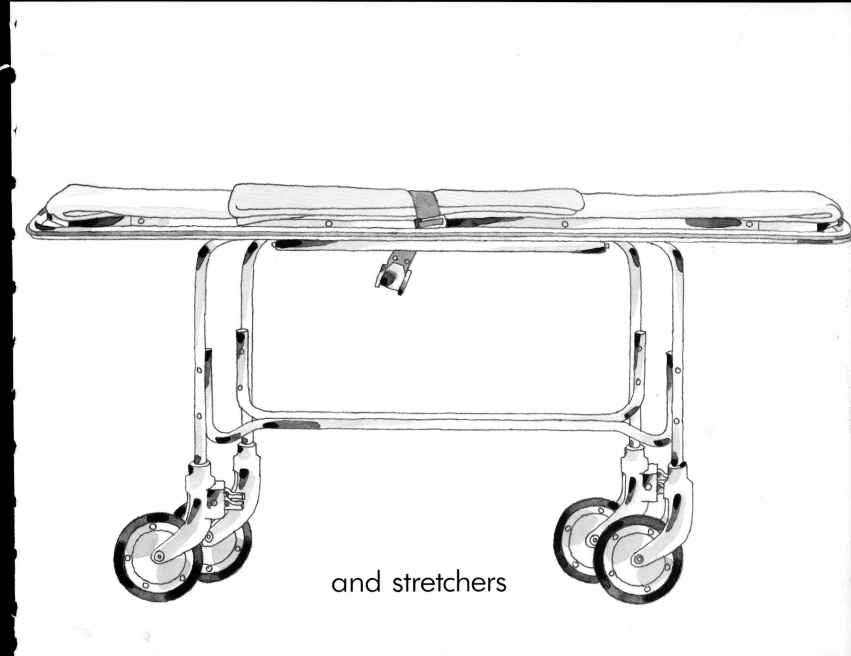

and stretchers

X-RAY →

for people
who are hurt or sick
to ride.
I rode in a wheelchair
when I sprained
my ankle.

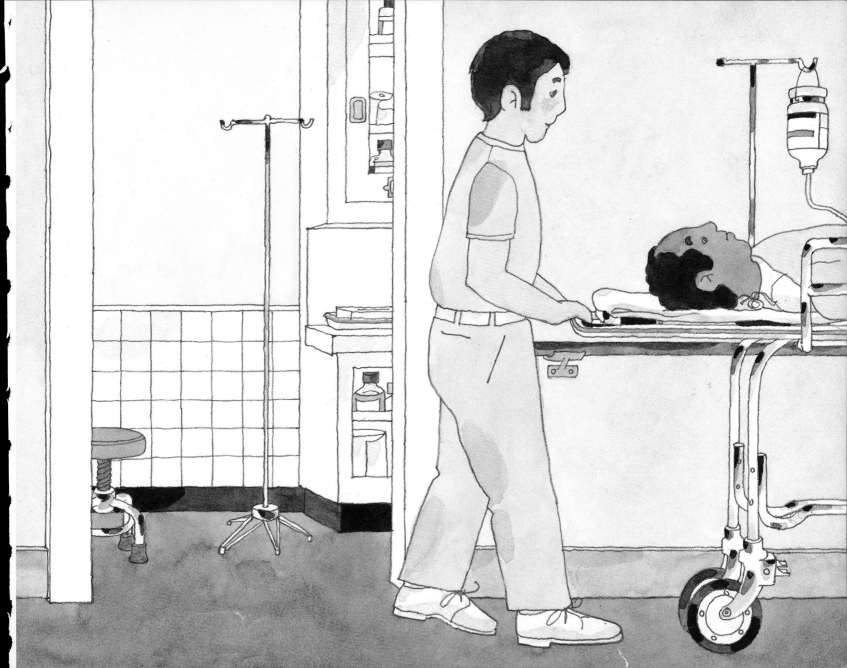

There are a lot of things in the emergency room. This tank holds oxygen for people to breathe.

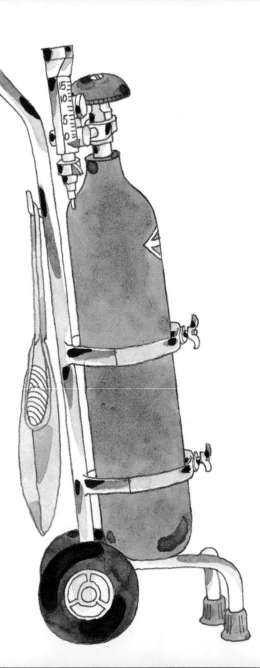

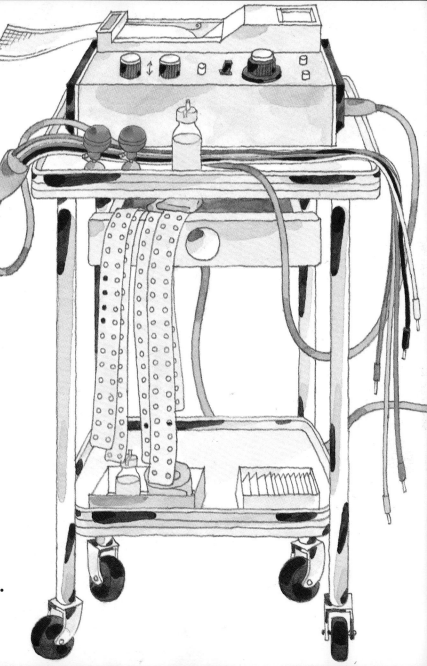

This machine shows
how a heart is beating.

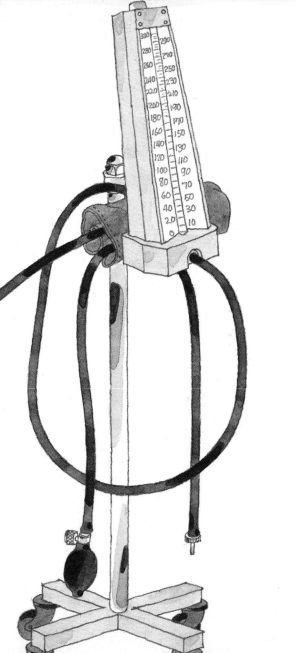

This instrument
measures blood pressure.
It rolls on wheels.

There are big sinks
where the nurses
wash cuts and bruises,
and bright lamps
so the doctors can look
at where it hurts.

There is an x-ray camera
in a special room.
I lay still
on the long metal table
while the camera
took a picture
of the bones in my ankle.

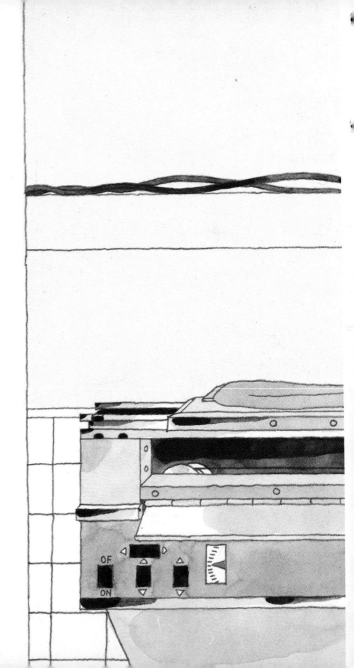

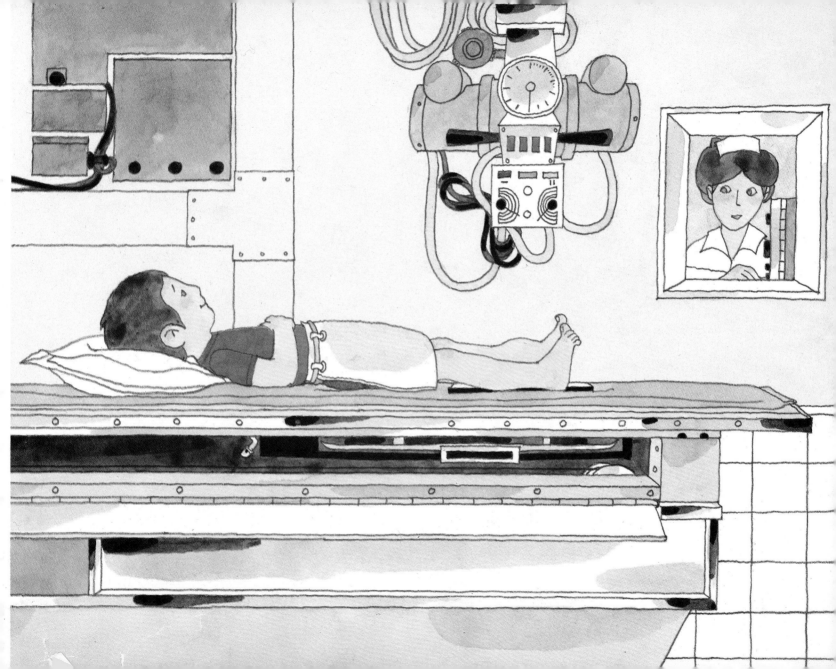

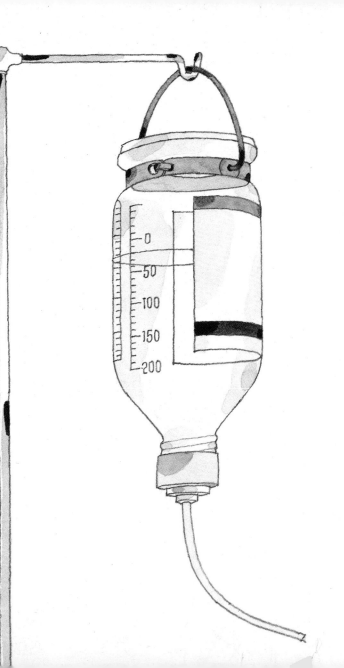

This big glass bottle
holds medicine that drips
into sick people's veins.

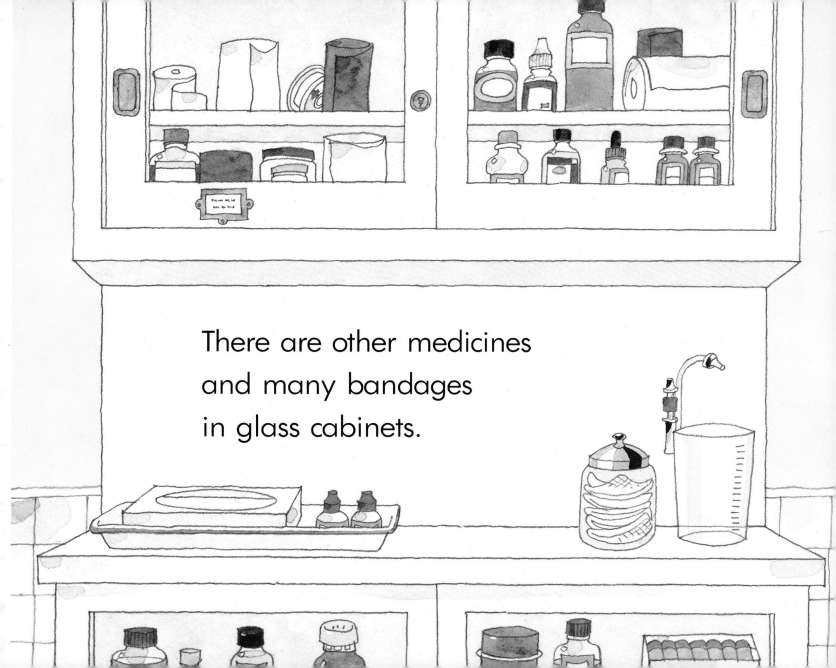

There are other medicines
and many bandages
in glass cabinets.

Doctors use little butterfly bandages
to close up cuts.

They use special bandages
for sprained ankles and broken bones.
The bandages are soft and wet
when the doctor puts them on.
But they make a hard plaster cast
when they are dry.

There are canes
and walkers
in the emergency room.
They help people to walk.

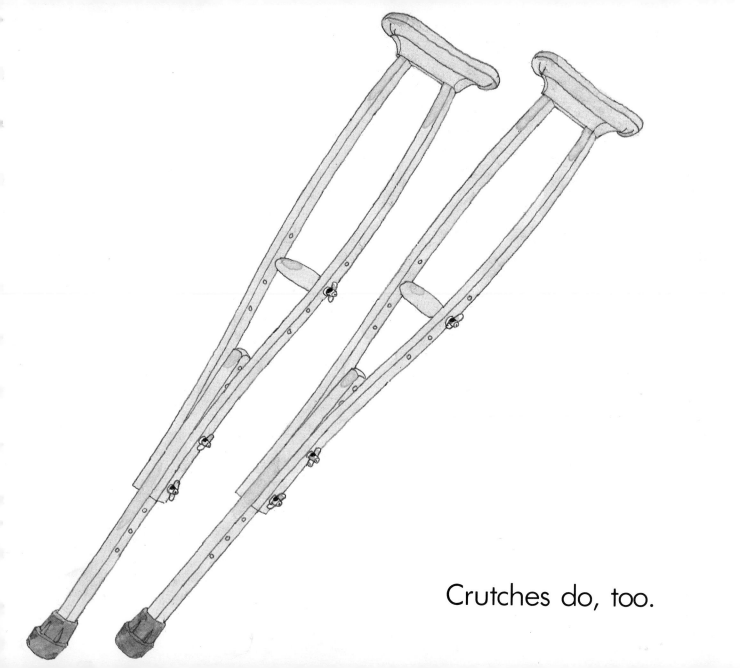

Crutches do, too.

I could not stand
on my sprained ankle.
So the nurse gave me crutches
and showed me
how to walk with them.

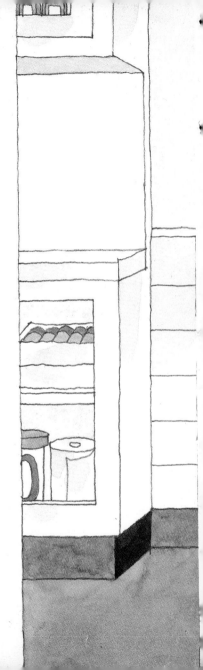

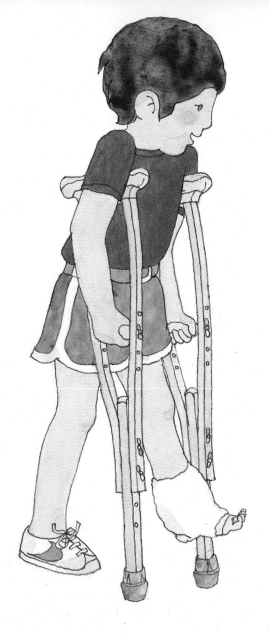

I walked
out of the emergency room
on my crutches,
and then I went home.